Better Days

(A Collection of Silent Poetry. By: Alexander Rodríguez)

Acknowledgements

This book is dedicated to every person that at some point wanted to get something off their chest. I also dedicate this book to all my friends and family. The support I've gotten from everyone is beyond words, so thank you. Lastly, I'd like to dedicate this book to the one and only Edgar Allen Poe. He made it easy for me to get lost in his words and inspired me to be a poet. May his work live on and continue to inspire others to think outside the box and get out of their comfort zone.

A Special Thank You to The Following People.

Maria Serrano
David Skoundrianos
Edward Skoundrianos
Tony Rodriguez
Carmen Rodriguez
Eddy Rodriguez
Kim Rodriguez
Anika Trujillo
John Polo
Cynthia Odeneal Brewer
Cecilia Goudanis
Edgar Munoz
My Poker Crew
Esmeralda Alvarez
Michael Anthony Chuqui
Alex Trujillo
Jocelyn Rodriguez
Michael Rodriguez
David Rodriguez
Maria Lily Hernandez

"Deep into that darkness peering, long I stood there, wondering, fearing, doubting, dreaming dreams no mortal ever dared to dream before."

- Edgar Allen Poe -

Introduction

Freshmen year in High School I picked up my first poetry book written by Edgar Allen Poe. It was a collection of short stories and poems. I remember not ever wanting to put the book down because of how good it was. As a matter of fact, I loved it so much that it was given to me by my teacher at the end of the school year.

When I was a Senior, I was given a project in English class which was to make a book and add it to our portfolio. This is when and where the idea of Silent Poetry was born. The concept of Silent Poetry was to make a book with as many poems as I could without telling anyone about it and surprising them when I finally decide to push it out.

Years had passed and I found my High School project. I decided that it was time I finally pushed it out for the world to enjoy except, I wanted to start over since I was a different person at this point in my life.

The Book you're about to read is a book full of pain, anger, happiness, love and my love for space. The thought of my thoughts being out there, open for the whole world to see is a scary thing. Especially because I'm putting thoughts out there in a way that I've never done so before. I feel vulnerable yet accomplished

Table of Contents

Table of Contents

Table of Contents

Table of Contents

Better Days

(A Collection of Silent Poetry. By: Alexander Rodríguez)

Empty

There's so much I want to tell you.
I wish you would've stuck around.
I've done so much without you.
I should carry a smile,
but there's none to be found.
I'm living the dream. I wish you could see me.
I want you to join me, but that might come off as needy.
I'm truly not sure how to feel.
I'm lost in my emotions.
I'm scared, I'm angry, I'm happy, and I'm sad.
I'm empty

Lost

Lost in my own demise and I don't seem to really mind.
Living the good life, tanning with the moonlight.
I wish I could explain everything to you.
You just wouldn't understand.

Once Upon a Time I Loved Her

She was made to be loved but she could never find it.
She couldn't find love even if she stood behind it.
Although, there once was a time when I actually loved her.
She captured my heart, we left life behind us.
Time was irrelevant when she was tied up in my arms. I had so much love for her, I could love her from afar.
An eternity of love was spent on her.
How the fuck could I be so stupid to mad love her. All that for nothing. What the fuck was I thinking?
She left me cold-blooded and it's just now starting to sink in.
Reality punched me on the face and left me on the floor bleeding with two busted eyes, a broken heart, and my ass sleeping.
But now, I'm wide awake.
Two months later, I realized this was fake.
Congratulations, my love, yeah, very well-played.
You left me so broken-hearted with no doctor to operate.
I wish I was warned your lips were poison; I would have never kissed them.
Now, I stand here alone as a grown man with my thoughts feeling conflicted.
And where are you now? You're nowhere to be found.
You're so lost in your bullshit, not even your shadow comes around.

Lose Lose and Lost

I dissected my thoughts by the handful. One by one they each got the
scalpel. Some got crucified for being martyrs.
I guess they still hold onto God.
The ones that slipped away got thrown in the wishing well, one at a
time, all just to wish you well.
They see something that I don't,
but these thoughts kill me all the time when I'm alone.
The mind is a horrible prison.
It's always me versus my thoughts. How the fuck could I ever win?

Fake in You

I'd like to bathe
with the fake in you,
wash it all away.
I think I might save you.
Look me in the eyes,
tell me you love me (lie).
I'll take the fake in you and watch it all die.
Now, tell me you're in love again.
Well, I don't believe you.
There goes the fake again.
I'm here to stay with you.
Wasting my time,
but for you I don't mind.
I'd like to bathe
with the fake person you hide.
Cold nights get lonely,
and you're warm if you care to ask me.
I would love to move on,
but you feel good in my arms.
with you, I have no secrets,
Like I'm made of glass.
Everything I hate about myself; you see right past.
You clean up my ugly and, like the sun, I dry you out.
I forget who I am sometimes,
but you remain my girl.
I'd like to bathe
with the fake that's inside of you,

Wash it all away.
I think I might save you.
Look me in the eyes, Tell me you love me (lie).
I'll take the fake in you and watch it all die.
Look me in the face. I'm a dying breed.
Look me in the eyes,
Tell me you're in love with me (lie).
I see the fake in you. Do you need me?
I see the fake in you. Don't you leave me.

Waiting on a Ghost

You want to avoid all kinds of hurt,
so you spend all your time killing emotions.
You're empty inside, no bones to your skin.
As dark as it is outside, you feel the same within.
You try to separate your heart from all kinds of happiness.
Tell me: How the hell is that working out so far?
You can't stop the pain; It's thirsty for the hurt.
Give in, put it to work.
You're not this love's slave. You don't owe it a damn thing.
Set yourself free and, when you're done, come save me.

New Company

I no longer say "goodbye." Now, I greet her at home.
The shadows that keep me company at night are no longer my own.
I've been waiting far too long for someone to put up with all my shit.
I had to compose myself. I just needed a clear definition of my
thoughts.
My hands were tied behind my back,
But you were in reach. You cut me some slack. We kissed in bliss.
Your saliva turned to wine. Get drunk off your kisses? I think I just
might.
Now we're here and things feel strange.
I hope we're okay. I hope things don't change, but if they did, I
couldn't blame you.
It's always my fault. I'm the fuck-up. Yeah, I fuck shit up.
I put myself through hard times.
Things are always hard when you're on my mind.
You might as well just count me out.
Love is never present, like rain to a drought.
If you cross my mind, stay for a while.
I won't mind killing time for as long as you want to.

The Stars

The stars are out now, closer than I could ever imagine.
They refuse to align for me, scattered all over like a fucking disaster.
It's like my body is polarized differently with great magnitude.
These stars keep pushing away from me, all with a bigger attitude.
One loss right after another. Not sure why I still bother.
I feel like I've been fighting for no reason.
I should charge myself with treason for going against all that I
believe in.
My tears keep getting heavy, Each one with a different story,
Each one with a different beginning,
Each one with pain that's never-ending,
Each one with different scars, different bruises.
It's a different day, but the same ol' bullshit.
I'm tired.
I think I just really need a break;
I think I'm ready to break.
But if the stars are down here, then I should go to space,
crawl into a black hole so that I don't have to live through this any-
more. I'll take all my fears with. I'll take a bucket to catch all my tears
with. Fuck it. I'll take all my shit because you won't be able to handle
it.
No matter how many times I try, I could never forget.
But I know I can start over.
Catch me on the shuttle next to Rover.
Send me to where I belong. Crash on a crater in Dimidium then
maybe I'll be left alone.

Been So Long

"Keep an open mind," she said.
Not sure what she wants.
Should I keep my guard up, babe? Or should I put away my heart?
Not sure how I'll feel when, when she finally comes around.
I might lose my shit, babe, but bad things crash and burn. It's been
so long now, so long. It's been so long now, so long. It's been so long
now, so long.
And now you're gone.

Daydreaming

Lost in my daydream.
Everything seems right to me. Making love to an illusion, so peaceful
and heavenly.
Cruising the outer space, far beyond the Milky Way, where no one
can find me.
Nothing here is random but me.
I'm the boy lost in a galactic space city.
Alien life is very aware.
They fear my thoughts but love my smooth skin.

Fear

Lost in life's tragedies,
I'm fighting a war I cannot win.
Nothing's real but pain now, and the fears I hide within.
Too much time spent by myself, lost in the dark, I'm all alone.
I'm not sure just how to feel, but this pain is much too real!
Memories are trapped in me; Memories I can't forget.
Blurry to my heart I cannot see. This fucking pain took over me.
I forgot what love felt like.
Too much hate consumed inside.
Tear this shit right out of me.
This fear I have dies here with me. I guess I lost track of who I was.
I guess I forgot how to move on. I guess I forgot to say good-bye.
Fuck!
I'll miss my family!

Lost in Forever

Demons, they want me.
Angels are crying.
I'm constantly changing, with nothing remaining.
All part of an illusion,
To offset, start confusion,
but really, I'm hiding, contemplating on dying.
It's pitch-black all around me.
Rip the shades off clouds above me.
I'm patiently waiting to take in all of my blessings.
God is fucking slacking, clueless of what's happening.
I need help, come and save me. Lost my mind, I'm going crazy.

No Grief

Like a beautiful summer's day
I don't know you anymore.
I need you to go away.
We've been here before.
You're a stranger to my eyes.
Pack up and leave.
I just want you to die.
I'll leave you with no grief.
Most people have dark clouds.
Well, I have you over my head.
I wear you so proudly.
But if you only knew
your thunder's so loud
and I hate the new you.

Nothing There

I wake up in the morning, feeling sad and lonely.
I turn on the hot water, jump into the shower,
Close my eyes and there you are, standing in front of me.
I inhale through my nose just to smell you.
I reach out just to touch you,
But you're gone and there's nothing there,
not even the mist of the hot water is in the air.
Where did you go?

Nowhere to Go

So, I run and hide and turn away,
but I find myself being stuck again.
So I think I might burn all my bridges.
Imagine life and living in the trenches.
So peaceful and calm, like the moon in the night,
lonely and cold.
Things will never be right.

Pain

You don't know pain like I know her.
She's always there to hold me when I don't need her.
She's my sunshine at night when I'm trying to sleep.
She's the black cat crossing my path when I walk the streets.
Wherever I go, she follows.
A heartbreak today, but something new tomorrow.
I hurt for her; she yearns for me. She spreads herself so willingly.
Well, I don't care if it hurts. I need to have some sort of control.
Give me back my emotions, stop draining my soul.
Every night I pray, "God, please take away my pain."
Not really sure what to say,
but every night I pray, "God, please bring me back my pain."

Past Me

I know you're out there, somewhere, suffering,
trapped in my mind, waiting to be set free.
Caught in your own demise.
Without you, I couldn't function inside, So I can't let you go.
I don't want to be left alone. Stay, build yourself a kingdom,
be the queen I need you to be.
Look past the haze. Look past everything,
except, past me.

Searching for Something

Every room I step in feels like a cage.
Every step I take moves me further away.
I'm lost in a city that has no God.
It's not where I want to be, but it's where I belong.
I'm searching for Jesus. Got scuffed-up knees.
Come, take me now, and bury me.
I'm ready for you.
Get off your cloud and look at me now.
I'm waiting for you.

Cruise

You make that dress look so new,
with a frown on your face that I've never seen before.
Come on, let's fool around; jump on top of me.
Ride this like a wave, one that will never come back ever again.
You let me cruise all your curves and I get away.
Lost in your body's gang way but who cares?
The moon has never looked so beautiful from this close
and I'm yours tonight, so come on, let's ride.
Clear your mind, get lost in time, tonight,
I'm yours, and tonight you're mine.

Midnight Cry

At midnight, I hear her crying. She won't let me sleep.
Her tears fall so hard to the floor, they sort of scare me.
I wish I understood her pain, then maybe I could help her.
Her feelings are ghostly; she's the apparition that haunts me.
Her silhouette is so beautiful, it shines as bright as a solar eclipse.
I wish I could look at her directly, but I'm too smart for that shit

Missing You Every Day

This is driving me crazy.
Bad thoughts keep following me.
I'm not sure what's going on.
I have night-sweats when I sleep.
I wake up with tears on my face.
I look for you, but you're not at my place.
You're at your mother's home.
Reality hits me: I'm all alone.
You're the key to the lock of my heart.
Without you, I'm torn apart.
I miss your smile and your stinky feet.
I miss you so much.
Please come back to me.

Behind Closed Doors

I'll be bae and you'll be baby.
I can make you feel good all over, if you only let me.
I'll hold you close and cover you in my skin,
To hide the broken bones from the damage you hold within.
Close your eyes, so we can travel for a moment,
I'll take you to the moon, so save your breath.
You'll have to hold it.
I could fuck you all night on the dark side of the moon.
I could bust a nut right inside of you.
I can make you hurt in all the right ways, if you allow it.
It'll take some time, but I'm sure you'll start to like it.
Before you know it, you won't bother to put up a fight.
You'll gladly give me your pussy, but we both know it's already mine.
I know that you're fragile, so I'll handle you with care,
I won't hurt you; I'll just stick you in with all my affairs.
Yeah, that means you're mine, and that means I'm yours.
That means whatever happens on the moon,
stays behind closed doors.

Come Back to Me

Today, I feel like I'm falling apart.
You've been on my mind for far too long.
Today, I'll miss holding you.
The demons inside me cry, it's true.
And I,
I must admit, being without you today feels like shit.
And I'm here, once again, oblivious to what's happening.
I refuse to submit, no, I'm not giving in,
but I want you back again, right by my side.
I see you all the damn time when I close my eyes.
I miss your smell; I miss your touch.
I miss your voice and all the above.
Come back to me. Come back to me.
At least I had you and no longer have to wonder.
All I have to do is hold onto you and remember.
Come back to me, come back to me soon, because tomorrow,
you'll be all alone.

Glory Hole

Oh, hello, my love. How are you doing?
You want to say "hi" to my friends? Well, come with me.
This is Anger, this is Pain, this is Lust, and this is Shy.
This one is Super-nice. She'll let you cum inside.
Wipe that look off your face!
It's time to meet Happy.
She's new to this place and was in the back room, napping.
She said she feels lonely and that makes her sad.
She must be bipolar. Let's put her back.
She was never consistent, so forget about her.
Let's say "hi" to Anger. Never mind.
Not sure what's gotten inside her.
All these friends of mine are all out of order.
Let's stick with Depression. You seem to know her.

Lovers Brawl

My hands on her throat, her legs on my shoulders. This is more than
just sex,
more than me wanting to fuck her.
No women's insides have ever wrapped so well around me.
So I thrust and I thrust. I want her to feel me. She screams loud like
thunder on a rainy day. I cum right inside her. She was my best lay.
She whispers in my ear, "You'll never be alone,"
But disappears like an apparition when the lights go on.

Muse

Now, I can't make sense of just what happened.
My arms guiding her straight to my lap and then she sat down on
me, starts to nibble on my ear.
She wants to get down and dirty, yeah, she wants to do it right here!
She's my kind of crazy. I think I fucking love her.
Let me take her to a place that we could never rest on.
We'll take an Uber to Jupiter. Surely it has a lot of vacant craters, or at
least one that we can fill both now and later.
I find it funny and cute she called me her muse
but she's the reason I put this pen and paper to good use. She's the
reason why I paint with the colors of the sky.
She's the reason why, with no wings, I want to fly.
She introduced me to something I've always longed for. Little does
she know this kind of love I would die for.

Come Get Me

I can't sleep, I'm anxious.
Bouncing off the wall, I'm right here just laughing, crying, hanging
off this edge.
I'm right here like
A statue, a pigeon. One more step,
I might trip and fall down. From right here, I'll turn around, so let
me in.
Come pin me down.
Don't go away.
Take me with you, or we'll go all the way.

Faultless Endearment

So meticulous, peculiar, and overzealous.
This crazy love has depression feeling so jealous.
Who would have thought this, Wrapped up in all my darkness?
The light, sometimes, it gets hard to see.
I almost missed you. You nearly slipped away from me.
I heard your cry, saw you draining both eyes, but give your tears to
the ocean tide.
What's wrong love? What's the problem?
Is it my vices?
Don't let my vices be so troublesome.
I'm as real as real can be. Pour your love all over me. Rest assured
that here I am.
Let your heart go wild. I don't give a damn.
Come, run into me.
Let the whole world see.
Let them witness something real: The passion, the love, the crazy,
the thrill.
Come, run into me.
Don't hold back. Just let it be. And when you go for a spin,
Just come back to me over and over again.

Love Is A Bitch

Your momma, your momma has me all wrong.
You know I'm a good boy and you can't be alone.
Time will continue to pass us by.
Two daggers to the heart. Why can't love just die?
I'm trying, I'm trying to keep my thoughts in good shape.
I can't stop thinking about you. There's always mind rape.
Flying, the winds brushing my face,
Looking for somewhere to land. In between your legs is a good place.
I need help, I need help with this sexual addiction.
Sex is not sexual enough without her submission.
I need to forget the taste of her lips;
Not the ones on her face, but the ones below her hips.
Say good-bye, say goodbye to everything you know.
I'll tie this ball and chain tight around your throat.
You need me. Take my heart and let's switch.
The shit I do for love. Yeah, love is a bitch.

Mindful of Me

It feels so good and it feels so right.
It feels so perfect for both you and I.
You're so magnificent,
with a love so pure and innocent.
How can I keep my mind at a distance?
I fell in love with you at first glance.
I want to hold you close to my chest.
I want to feel how hard your nipples get when I touch your breasts.
I want to touch your skin, glide my fingers down your spine, make
love to whatever tunes might come about if you don't mind.
I want to give you my broken heart.
Be mindful of all the broken parts.
I want to make love to you 'cause you're so lovely.
I want you to feel the same way.
Shit, I just want you to love me.
I'll hold you by the soul.
With me, you'll never be alone.

My Perfect Song

Sometimes, I close my eyes and picture you next to me.
I often wonder why I let the Devil get the best of me.
Sometimes, I feel like I'm lacking a few prayers. Sometimes, I feel
like I miss everything about her. Sometimes, I don't give a fuck and
I hope she dies. When I get these thoughts, I quickly open my eyes.
Why did it come down to this?
Why is this happening?
You told me God will take it away from me.
Well, here's proof, my new reality.
Sometimes, I feel so lost that I can't hide my emotions.
Even as I write these thoughts,
my eyes combust with explosions of tears out of my eyes.
I never imagined this kind of life,
but here I am now being forced to.
Sometimes, just sometimes,
I want to punch God in the face.
I want to give up and say,
"Fuck all of this shit. Fuck this stupid faith.
Fuck everything and anything that has to do with Him.
Fuck all your promises and blessings. Fuck it all with a passion,
Because following you has only gotten me my ass kicked."
Then, I close my eyes and picture you next to me.
I often wonder way I let the Devil get the best of me.
I can still smell you. I even spray your scent in the house.
I feel borderline crazy, but what the fuck do I know?
One thing's for sure: I'm still yours, and I hope you're still mine.
I pray this love of ours will heal all within time.
I wish you the best for now.
I pray you find someone that will take care of you the way you want.
Let me know if you need me. It was nasty at the end,
but you were mine from the start.
I have nothing but love for you, even if you can't see it.
You were the love of my life right from the beginning.

Jaded

I feel so over-jaded.
These demons of mine feel so overrated.
Let's remove myself from these emotions.
Let's remove the weight of the world from both of my shoulders.
It's time to fix my balance by fixing my posture.
Time to put the pussy away. Bring back the monster.
Time to stand up for myself because you no longer stand with me.
Time to occupy the seat of the queen that sits next to me.
Time to bring out the sunshine and put the messy away.
Time to start a new life, and it starts today.
There's no heartbreak if the heart doesn't ache.
There's no heartbreak if the heart is fake.

Gone

Who are you?
What have you become?
Why did you take your life through the barrel of a gun?
That's figuratively speaking because you're still physically here.
You just took the image I had of you and made it disappear, replaced it with an imposter. Someone else.
A figment of your imagination. Someone false.
A distorted you in full capacity.
Has me oblivious to the world and this crazy city.
I shed a tear for you every day.
It drips down my eyes, right off my face.
But this time, I'll store it in my pocket, the one close to my heart, and I'll lock it.
Right next to the grain of salt for all the shit you keep fucking up.
I have so many memories flashing in my head.
I wonder, do you believe all the bullshit that you've said?
The reality is, I never really knew you,
But did you even know you? Does anyone even know you?
Who the fuck takes the credit for all your animosity?
All the shit you do and say. What the fuck were you thinking?
What happened to "till death do us part"?
When did that become "till you no longer give a fuck"?
All your temperamental temperaments caused by outside elements.
Things that shouldn't even play a role in this equation, but you let them right in and let them take over.
Now it's twelve years down the drain, twelve years later and we have to start over.
I hope these next twelve years help you ease the pain when you finally decide to come over.
But I guess I should take my losses and run.
I should become like you and make myself gone.

Clad Up, Lovers

Wrap your mind around me.
I'll take your mind off everything. I'll be your mind-fuck for a while.
I'll even give it to you raw. I'll dress you in my thoughts,
and take the blame for all those sins.
You make it all worth it, even the eternal pain.
So, I'll be your destruction. I'll be your cleaning crew. I'll be your
distraction.
All you need that's pure.

Don't You Give In

I incarcerated these demons of mine.
They've been with me for a while doing just fine.
Locked up behind my prison walls.
They've broken jaws, chewing through these iron bars.
Their toothless smiles are so hard to ignore.
They taunt me and taunt me. With a punch, I lay them out to the floor.
They've been sexually deprived for quite so long, eyeballing each other, closely waiting for the soap to fall. Down each other's throats, dogpile one after another.
Too desperate for love, they no longer bother.
Let me out, Alex! Let me out now!
I'd gladly let you out, demons, but I don't know how.
Why don't you give in? Why don't you give in? My eyelids are heavy, and knees are shaking.
I fall to the floor and gouge my eyes out.
They found a way out. My world is starting to die now.
They don't need me no more, need me no more.
My world has been shaken; my heart fell to the floor.
Once you give in, the damage begins. Once you give in, the damage begins. Once you give in, no more suffering.

Give Me You

I'm a piece of shit, and there you stand, so perfect.
I take pride in your joy, yeah, it's so worth it.
You're an angel that fell from the sky, with broken wings, there's no
way you can't fly.
But here I stand, in awe, so peaceful.
Staring at you, Not at your flaws,
Just at your perfection.
Connecting your birthmarks has become an obsession.
You must be what life is like.
Let me drink you because I feel dead inside.
Bring me back to life. Revive me.
Breathe into my mouth. I want you inside me.
Give me your joy, your peace, and your comfort. Give me whatever
it is that you stand for.
I want it all. I want your everything.
I want to keep you for myself.
You're just right for me.

Heal the Broken

Can you see the sky? It's starting to cry. Can you take my filth and
learn to ride? Can you see my pain? It's seeping through.
Can you take this broken-spirited man and make him new?
Don't you see your lips? They miss me so much.
Don't you want me to kiss you in places that don't blush?
Don't you know you can't swim? You'll drown in the ocean of your
lies.
Don't you see what you've become? A pile of shit surrounded by
maggots and flies.
I'm looking for a new beginning, but bitterness drips from my pores.
I want you to give me back what's mine, and you can take back what's
yours.
I hope you know we're losing daylight and time is going by.
I hope you know everyone is moving along and everything is just
fine.

Like Father, Like Son

Dummy boy, stupid kid.
Look at you, a fucking misfit.
You stand alone, nobody likes you.
My heart breaks for you. That's not true.
I wonder, what will you make of yourself in the future?
Why do you let everything I say get to you?
I'm trying to make you a man. Don't think I'm insane. I want to take
your life and put it in a picture frame.
I hope you enjoy all my negativity.
I hope all this bullshit makes you want to be just like me.
When I grow old and I die, I want you to thank me,
I know there were times you would have much rather the spanking.
That won't teach you a thing. It'll only make you weaker. I could only
show that I loved with poison to your ears.
I'm sorry, big boy. I wish I wasn't like this.
I wish my parents were there when I needed a hug and a kiss.
Maybe my words wouldn't hurt you so much. I really couldn't tell
you.
I just want you to know from the bottom of my heart, son, I really
love you

Love Is Hate

I'd be lying if I told anyone I didn't hate you. A part of me will always love you effortlessly. A part of me kills you every night, indefinitely.

Misled

These feelings get old and soon, they'll fade away.
I blame it all on you, so please go away.
I've lost all good thoughts. You flushed them down the drain.
You have filled my life with rain and pain. So far, I think I
can do well without you, But this time, I'll be the one to flush
you. Where? Down. Where? The. Where? Drain.
Where?
Down the drain.

My Unicorn

You don't like the silence and you never will. You hold fast to the violence for the cheap thrill.
That's my kind of crazy. I won't coerce you to change.
You're perfect just the way you are, I know, 'cause I'm the same.
Two peas in a pod, they say. That sounds like shit. My bitch and your dog! Now that's more like it.
So, how well do you know chance? Well, I'm not sure you know it.
If you really did know chance, you'd grab its dick and blow it.
Tell me where you've been because I haven't heard from you in a minute.
This ride I'm on is full of crazy, and you're missing out on it.
I'll let you take a ride on opening up and hopefully you spill your guts.
I couldn't care less if you're crazy.
I want to know you're fucking nuts!

Love

Love is an intense feeling of deep affection.
Love is good in all the right ways.
But love is dark. Love is horrible. Love is rage.
Love died the day you rattled my cage.
Now I hate you.
Now I can't stand you.
I would spit in your face, but my saliva is too good for you.
P.S. I love you.

I'll Be the Reason

I'll be the reason you won't talk at night.
I'll be the reason the neighbor stomps on the floor, ready to fight.
I'll be the reason you scream and shout.
I'll be the reason the cops pay a visit to the house.
I'll be the reason you wake up with bruises all over your body.
I'll be the reason you won't settle for just anybody.
I'll be the reason people will ask if you're okay.
I'll be the reason people are concerned for your safety every day.
I'll be the reason your friends won't see you as much.
I'll be the reason you brace yourself after a touch. I'll be the reason
you will get numbed to the pain. I'll be the reason you crave it over
and over again.
I'll be the reason you're addicted to hurting. I'll be the reason you ask
for more again.

Utopia

I want to create another time, another place, somewhere parallel to
Earth with only beings, no race.
Somewhere I could start my own religion. Everyone is God.
Fuck having nothing here; you'll have it all.
The weak will be unaware of all their surroundings.
It'll be for the best. That's the only way they'll be able to survive.
You won't understand it, but that won't matter.
As a matter fact, you won't give a fuck because you are God,
and Gods tend to do whatever the fuck they want.
While everyone is "God," you can call me "Lord." I'll watch over
everyone like no one's ever watched before.
I'll keep our little world safe.
I'll create a cancer in case it overpopulates.
You'll try to put up a fight,
but you'll become an enemy of mine.
I'll charge you with treason.
I'll cut your head off with no valid reason, Because I am Lord, and I
tend to do whatever the fuck I want!

Weakness

I'll carve my name onto your chest just to hear you squeal.
You'll wear it proudly under your red dress once it starts to heal.
I know it's beneath all your filthy swag.
I've wasted too much time caught up in your ugly trap.
Stuck there, I've committed to all your beatings.
It wasn't hard for you, since you knew my weakness.
Now, I've found a way to get out and ahead.
I spent so much time on perfecting it.
You're going to miss me once the dust starts to settle.
I'll keep my guards up in case you're ready for another battle.

Used To

I can get used to hearing these sirens, breaking the law, making a big
mess. I could get used to all the violence,
the biting, the scratching. It all feels so nice.
I can get used to dancing with crazy, kissing your neck, grabbing
your ass.

Beg

I can see you giving up. I can see me losing it all.
Where are you? Show me the light. Let go of the hate you hold inside.
Give me hope, show me this stands for something. Open your heart,
open your legs, and let me jump in.
Put on this blindfold, snap on these cuffs. Your pain is my pleasure.
I can't get enough.
I know that you think without me, you'll be fine. But no one else will
take the chance to give you life.
Your heart's broken, but I'll fix it.
I'll make you look good with red lipstick
and black nylon. I'll make you beg for it all night long.

What If

Once upon a time, you jumped into my life.
You stayed and fell asleep. Your body was all over mine.
Your scent crept into my pores,
but you knew from the beginning I was always yours.
We made out, I breathed you in,
I found love through you once again. What if all of this was never
true?
What if you never came to my rescue?
I would never find myself in you.
Now, you decide what to make of this.
Is it true love or a simple fuck(ing) kiss? Well, right now, I don't want
to know.
I just want to have dinner under the cosmos.
Let the sound waves in our Solar System crash on our eardrums.
Let's dance to the beat of our newfound love.
Kiss these rusted, old lips, lubricate them with your sweet saliva.
Kiss me till the flame goes down, till there is no longer a fire.

What Did You Do to Me

Who would have thought this? These thoughts are so thoughtless.
How could I love her so fearlessly?
How can I be so naive to think she was meant for me?
Be still. You just want to steal my broken heart.
Where did she come from? How did she steal my heart?
She manifested from childish thoughts.
Now, she has me silly with a childish heart.
This crazy love is so belligerent.
I want to keep loving her over and over again.
I want to kiss her all over her body. I want to feel her love all over me.
I want to bathe in her sex sweat.
I want her juices to drip down my mouth when her pussy is wet.
When it comes to loving her, I'll be an over-achiever.
I won't fuck this up because I want to keep her.
I love you so much, I want to fuck the particles around you.
I love you some much, I want to impregnate the bacteria around you.
I love you so much, this can't be real. I love you so much, I want to
feel you.

Summer Baby

You're running out of time. Summer baby, please be mine.
Tomorrow will bring the rain. I don't want to lose you again.
Summer baby, please come back to me.
You're running out of time. Why can't you see?
Winter's almost mine.

The Dissolvement

As my words draw you away, our faith together reeks of piss. And
our hearts, they fade to black Over all the BS we intake.
Now we're here and it's come down to this.
Your lips dodge my kiss.
Deeper and deeper is every cut.
You cut and you cut without giving a fuck.
Who would have known?
Now you, me, and our hearts are all alone.

The Empty Part of My Heart

I walked away and made it safe, just like you knew I would.
I'm so sorry you broke my heart. Guess we were just misunderstood.
In the next life, I promise you'll have my undivided attention,
because in this lifetime, it's over with no room for redemption.
But there's a place in my heart that you can borrow. You can stay
there. You'll be safe, at least for a while.

The Right Kind of Pain

I want to fuck you from dusk till dawn.
I want to lick you from toe to head.
I want to suck you dry when you're soaking wet.
I want to swim in the ocean of cum in between your legs.
I want to drink your juices for breakfast in bed.
Dig your claws into my back, cut me open from the outside.
Lick me, bit me, scratch me. I won't mind that.
With the matchbook on the counter,
I will light the candle to drop hot wax on her. I'll choke her to death,
at least for a moment.
She'll probably think I'm crazy, but I'll just ignore her. She'll throw
me off guard when she yells out for more.
Ass in the air and face to the floor.

The Taste of Steel

Your tears don't want to be shed. So long to sadness; this is its end.
Kiss the Tin Man goodnight, Savor the metallic taste.
That'll be the last time anything touches your face. Remember to say
your good-byes and so-longs.
Soon you'll be right where you belong.

The Trap

The Devil loves rejects.
He lures them one by one. What'd you expect?
He calls them by their sin, not their name.
"Hello, adulterer, let me in. I have the remedy to stop your pain.
Listen to no one but hear me out.
I'll remove all of your doubts."
The Devil doesn't play, so don't listen to him.
Remove yourself from the dark before he locks you in.

The Traveler and His Wife-to-Be

I drove a spaceship over to Mars.
I came across a lot of beautiful Martians. Then, I saw you and it kept
me in awe.
Your presence stopped me right were my heart is.
Somehow, I knew it belonged to you, but you didn't want to take it.
I wasn't sure what to do.
So, you pushed me away, you didn't want to break it.
Something about you feels so familiar.
You're the girl in my dreams.
She needs to swallow me so I can be inside her.
You're the dark shadow looking over me.
Stand still like the ocean in the dark.
Come to me, my love, enjoy my presence. Watch over me like a child
watches the stars. Where I'm taking you, you'll feel restless.
So, come to me, my love. Get ready to love me.
Let's get married somewhere on Mars.
I need you to want me.

The Wait

She goes where the wind suggests she goes.
I turn on my fan. Take a deep breath in, one so deep it
over-capacitates my lungs.
I blow. I blow and I blow. Harder and harder with every breath I take,
I blow.
All in hopes that the wind I blow suggests she comes my way.
I know that sounds stupid and, realistically, it will never happen, but
I really don't care. I'll still blow for as long as
I have lungs. I mean, what's the worst that could happen? For all I
know, one day, she might just come home to me.

These Demons of Mine

Your words are so cryptic. You speak in tongues, but I understand it
when no one else does.
I will follow you until we feel God's wrath.
Nothing will harm you or even cross our paths. Those sins of yours,
they now belong to me.
He died for our sins, but only set you free.
I remain a slave to myself. These demons hold me back, they keep me
in line when I fall off-track.
Who else but me would die for you? Everyone but me is ashamed of
you.
Hold onto my hand, grip it tight,
use both hands because slip you just might. Take shelter in the empty
spot of my chest. I would never let you go. I will let you rest.

Not Sure What That Even Means

Losing something is better than losing it all,
but I'm not sure what that even means.
Having a euphoric experience with you was a lifelong dream,
but I'm not sure what that even means.
I was very much so malleable. You just didn't apply pressure,
but I'm not sure what that even means.
Castigating me for the faults of my past,
but I'm not sure what that even means.
Look at me now, a lost nudnik around every couple,
but I'm not sure what that even means.
Acerbic to love and everything else,
but I'm not sure what that even means.

Obsession

I met a girl last night.
I really wanted to hate her. We got off to a good start. Now, things are complicated.
I like her and, yeah, she likes me, but I love you.
This is so confusing.
She's the difference between love and perfection.
I'm so obsessed.
Yeah, she's become my new obsession.

Once Upon a Punk

Let down your wall. Let me fill in your gap.
As crazy as I am, you know you'll like that.
I'll dress you in my cum.
You'll be bathing in my purity.
Grab yourself a glass and have a drink of my insanity.
You think I miss you?
Well, I miss your everything.
You're the punk I wish I had never met. You're the punk I fucked and
don't regret.
But you liked it, and so did I.
You made it hard for me to say "goodbye," So, I guess I'll just say, "see
you later." Fuck.
She stole my heart, when I just wanted to bang her.

Only in My Dreams

We still talk, only in my dreams, every night in my head.
I can't wait to talk to you tonight when I'm lying down in bed.
There's so much about me that I want to tell you:
Things that you never knew, things you wouldn't believe are true,
but they are. I dream about you a lot, and in my dreams, you actually
love me.
Yes, how funny is that? You actually love me.
Somehow, we get along. You came back.
The kids and both you and I are so fucking happy.
The crazy thing is that, even in my dreams, I know I'm dreaming.
I tell myself this is just a dream, but I refuse to wake up, because I'm
in utopia.
Now, how fucked up is that?

Over My Shoulder

Looking over my shoulders, he's right behind.
He took everything he wanted, even my wasted time.
Now I'm all alone with nowhere to go.
He took my shoes and made them his own.
It's a long way down and, of course, I'm scared. Looking over my shoulder and he's always there.
I fell flat on to my face once again. I need to get up.
Locked lips with the Devil. Now I'm his bitch and whatnot.
At the rate I'm going, Hell's around the corner.
I'm stuck in his confines now he's my owner. He's so far in my ear.
He won't leave me alone.
Playing the same tune over and over, beating on my eardrum.
Why did he come? He doesn't belong.
Let him taste the steel, so this could be done.
Let him taste the steel. I hate you.
So long.

Perfect

I'm far from perfect, but I don't give a shit.
I've learned to numb the pain and I perfected it.
With the mindset of a killer, blood stains covered all over my t-shirt.
The pictures on the wall: I've set them on fire, I've watched them
burn.
I've made some mistakes, but from them I've learned.
Exasperated with your presence,
I no longer want to be involved with this torment.

Picture Perfect

Look for the daylight and you'll find the way out.
Put away your vices. Those things no one should know about.
You're starting fresh, like a spring flower.
Wash the nasty away with a nice, hot shower.
You're new now, reborn again, just like you always dreamed of.
Right down to the T.
Picture perfect you, waiting on picture perfect me.
Well, picture perfect you, I'm not coming.
There's nothing picture perfect about you, nothing worth wanting.

Since You Left

Since you left and walked out of the door,
I hold onto something I never held onto before. I've tried to say my
peace on a piece of paper.
Thought writing would heal this broken heart, a little later, but I
never thought that I could be so fucking wrong.
You became the victim in all my fucked-up songs.
I've tried to make my peace with you,
But how can I make my peace if you don't allow me to?
Now, this me that I've become is someone you've never seen before.
With all the hurt you put me through, he wants to choke the shit out
you.
But I won't let him, because I'm your man in arms.
Come into my arms. You won't be alone.
Well, just so you know, this isn't a poem for you; it's an update, I just
want you to see I'm doing just great!

Slow Motion

Sometimes, the meaning of life is missing.
That's because nobody is listening. Too many demons and no con-
cerns. Take these broken-hearted maggots.
They're all yours.
My eyes are finally open.
I'll hold off on showing emotions, but you're ten galaxies away.
I'll hold my breath for the first two and suffocate for the next eight.
I feel like I'm moving in slow motion.
I have body damage from the cosmic ocean.
My eyes will be set on you. Stay in that spot, don't move.
I'm getting closer,
but I'm drowning in the ocean of your tears.
Come to me, I'm still here. I'm moving in slow motion.

Space Crusaders

So, if the darkest night produces the brightest stars, when I get laid,
it better be black-out, pitch dark.
You better strap on to a harness,
'Cause when I find you, I'm giving it one hundred.
Whisper sweet nothings in my ear.
Mumble all the nasty words you want me to hear.
Let's book a trip to Mars. I'll be the space captain.
I'll put on the fancy hat while you sit on my lap and enjoy the
beautiful view from the cosmic waves.
Go to sleep on Saturn's rings just to wake up tomorrow and do it
over again.

S.J. (Sarah-Jayne)

I'll let you in on a secret:
She drives me crazy. I want to keep her.
I want to take her to places I've never been.
I want to kiss her all over, just not sure where to begin.
She sets me on fire.
The fumes from her legs got me feeling higher.
I wouldn't mind taking her now.
Unfortunately, I won't be able to see her, at least not for a while.
This must be the shit Romeo felt when he and Juliet first met.
It's no wonder my words soak her in between, so wet.
Well, I'll be the one to fuck her soul first, because before me, she was
never yours.

Name

She forgot my name, and I forgot it too.
All this craziness keeps on pointing back to her.
It's okay; she belongs to me, like the moon to the wolf at night,
like the demons to hell, and the angels to the sky.
I sit here, holding it all inside.
Something is missing. I can't put a finger on it.
It's her; she's what's missing. Love won't let me forget about her.
I'm on my own, missing her deeply, regretting it all, choking up on
memories that once were ours, now barely mine.
I don't want to move forward; I want to hold back time.
Only you can drop me down to my knees.
The pain, the anger, the agony: take it all. It doesn't belong to me.
So long, my love, until we meet again,
Hopefully, the next time we meet, you'll remember my name.

Better Days

You're sure to let me down,
but it's okay. I can stand on my own.
I'm the master of my domain.
I've dreamed so much of better days.
Yeah, of better days. Things will get better someday. But, before
things get better, I have to taste the bitter.
Yeah, taste the bitter. The scent of cat piss in my mouth mixed with
cat litter.
Yeah, the taste of bitter. Man, do I wish I would've never met her.
Then I think of my beautiful kids and I want to thank her.
Yeah, I want to thank her. I close my eyes and pray all the time for
her.
Lord, please bless her. Yeah, Lord, bless her.
When she comes after you at night, please embrace her.
Yeah, embrace her. Let her know that everything will be okay. Yeah,
be okay. And with you, she will come to better days.

Apocalypse Shit

The world will shake, plate tectonics will break
and landfills will collapse.
Nothing was ever meant to last.
The Earth from space will look a lot brighter, when everything on
land is hiding under a fire.
The smoke will create stormy clouds. Lightning striking loud from
all around.
Spring will turn to fall, and the rain will drown us all.
Where is your God, where did he go?
He's been looking from above, down below.
I'm starting to think this is all my fault.
I should have never prayed for Earth to fall apart.
Now I can learn to appreciate and admire, all the things I lost in the
fire.

THE END

Better Days

(A Collection of Silent Poetry. By: Alexander Rodríguez)

Made in the USA
Columbia, SC
17 September 2019